THE
Haunted Hamburger

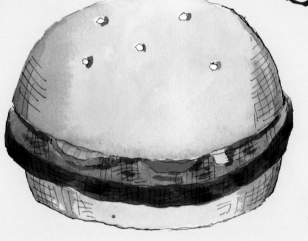

AND OTHER *Ghostly Stories*

BY **David LaRochelle**

ILLUSTRATIONS BY **Paul Meisel**

DUTTON CHILDREN'S BOOKS · *An imprint of Penguin Group (USA) Inc.*

To my parents, Ruth and Roger LaRochelle,
from their son who never wanted to go to bed

D.L.

For Sara Reynolds and Lucia Monfried, a wonderful team

P.M.

DUTTON CHILDREN'S BOOKS
A division of Penguin Young Readers Group

Published by the Penguin Group · Penguin Group (USA) Inc., 375 Hudson Street, New York, New York 10014, U.S.A.
Penguin Group (Canada), 90 Eglinton Avenue East, Suite 700, Toronto, Ontario M4P 2Y3, Canada (a division of Pearson
Penguin Canada Inc.) · Penguin Books Ltd, 80 Strand, London WC2R 0RL, England · Penguin Ireland, 25 St Stephen's
Green, Dublin 2, Ireland (a division of Penguin Books Ltd) · Penguin Group (Australia), 250 Camberwell Road, Camberwell,
Victoria 3124, Australia (a division of Pearson Australia Group Pty Ltd) · Penguin Books India Pvt Ltd, 11 Community
Centre, Panchsheel Park, New Delhi - 110 017, India · Penguin Group (NZ), 67 Apollo Drive, Rosedale, North Shore 0632,
New Zealand (a division of Pearson New Zealand Ltd) · Penguin Books (South Africa) (Pty) Ltd, 24 Sturdee Avenue,
Rosebank, Johannesburg 2196, South Africa · Penguin Books Ltd, Registered Offices: 80 Strand, London WC2R 0RL, England

Library of Congress Cataloging-in-Publication Data
LaRochelle, David.
The haunted hamburger and other ghostly stories / by David LaRochelle; illustrated by Paul Meisel.
p. cm.
ISBN 978-0-525-42272-3 (hardcover)
[1. Ghosts—Fiction. 2. Bedtime—Fiction. 3. Brothers and sisters—Fiction.
4. Humorous stories.] I. Meisel, Paul, ill. II. Title.
PZ7.L3234Hau 2011 · [E]—dc22 · 2010038179

Published in the United States by Dutton Children's Books,
a division of Penguin Young Readers Group
345 Hudson Street, New York, New York 10014
www.penguin.com/youngreaders

Designed by Sara Reynolds and Kristin Machado
Manufactured in China · First Edition
10 9 8 7 6 5 4 3 2 1

"Time for bed," said Father Ghost.

"But we are not tired," said Franny and Frankie.

"Tell us a story," said Franny.

"Tell us a scary story," said Frankie.

"If I tell you a story, do you promise to go to bed?" said Father Ghost.

Franny and Frankie crossed their fingers.

"We promise," they said.

"Very well," said Father Ghost. "But I must warn you. This is a very scary story. . . ."

The Scary Baby

One day your uncle Ned was flying down the street.

"I am in the mood to scare somebody," he said. He saw an old man reading the newspaper.

"Ha! That old man should be easy to scare. Boo!"

"Is it Halloween already?" asked the old man. "What a cute costume!" He patted Uncle Ned on the head and gave him a gumdrop.

Uncle Ned flew away. He did not like gumdrops, and he did not like to be called cute.

He saw a teenager walking down the sidewalk.

"I am going to scare the pants off that teenager," said Uncle Ned. "Boo!"

"Hey! That is my favorite song!" said the teenager. *"Boo-boo bam! Boo-boo bam! Boo-boo, boo-boo, boo-boo bam!"*

Uncle Ned covered his ears and flew away. He hated music.

He spotted an open window and flew inside. Lying in a crib was a little baby.

"At last I have found someone I can scare," he said.

"BOOOO!"

The baby opened her eyes.

"BOOOOOO!"

The baby opened her mouth.

"BOOOOOOOO!"

The baby reached out her tiny hands . . .
She grabbed Uncle Ned and began sucking on his sheet!
"Stop that!" screamed Uncle Ned.
The baby began to cry.

Your uncle Ned had never heard such a terrible noise. It was even worse than the teenager's singing. He flew into an open drawer to hide from the crying baby.

While he was hiding, he heard someone walk into the room.

"Poor baby," said the someone. "I bet you need to be changed."

"Good," thought Uncle Ned. "I hope they change that awful baby into a toad or a snake."

But that is not what happened.

Bwaaah!

Gwaaah

Waaah!

A hand reached into the drawer, grabbed Uncle Ned by his
sheet, and before he could fly away, your uncle had become . . .

A DIAPER!

A diaper!" screamed Franny and Frankie.

"That's horrible!" said Franny.

"That's terrible!" said Frankie.

"That's disgusting!" they both said.

"I told you it was a scary story," said Father Ghost. "Now climb into bed and go to sleep."

"But we are still not tired," said Franny.

"If you tell us another scary story, then we promise to go to sleep," said Frankie.

"Very well," said Father Ghost. "But I must warn you. This is a very, very scary story. . . ."

The Haunted Hamburger

"Your cousin Nell was a boastful ghost," Father Ghost said.

"I am the fastest ghost in the world!" said Nell.

"I am the smartest ghost in the world!

"I am the scariest ghost in the world!"

"Big deal," said her friend Lulu. "I know someone who is faster, smarter, and scarier than you. His name is the Haunted Hamburger. He lives in the Dark Forest. Why don't you go see him for yourself . . . unless you are too afraid."

"I am not afraid of anything," said Nell. "I am the bravest ghost in the world."

So Nell flew off to the Dark Forest to find the Haunted Hamburger.

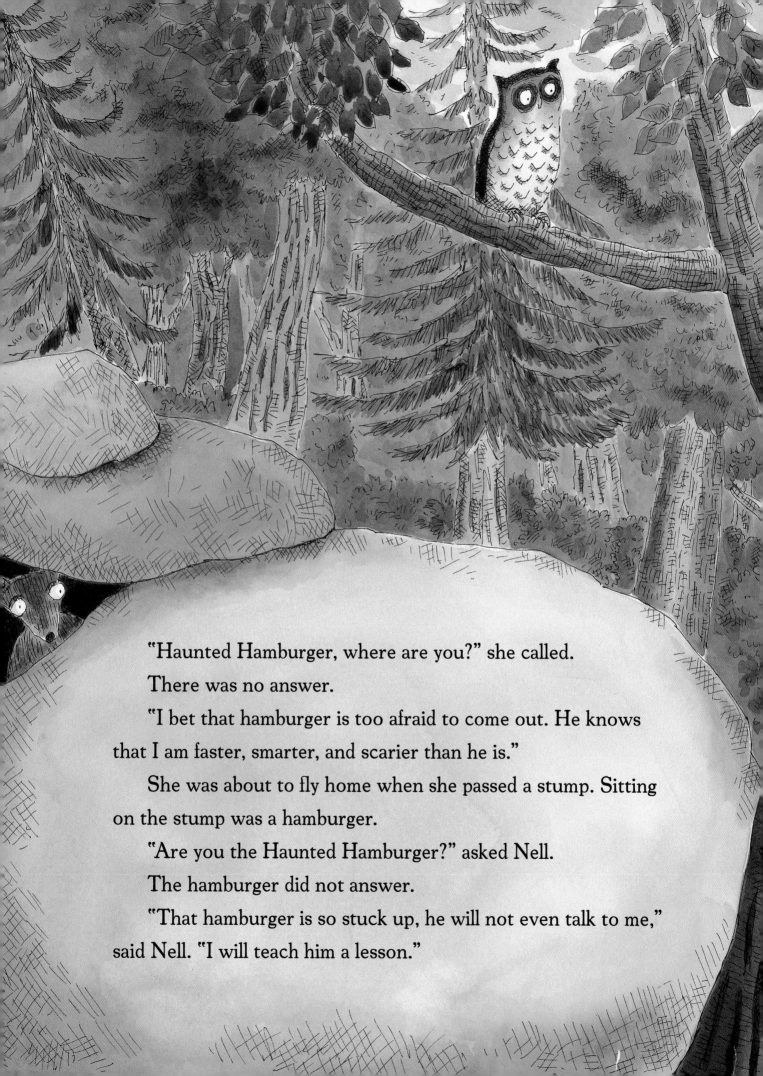

"Haunted Hamburger, where are you?" she called.

There was no answer.

"I bet that hamburger is too afraid to come out. He knows that I am faster, smarter, and scarier than he is."

She was about to fly home when she passed a stump. Sitting on the stump was a hamburger.

"Are you the Haunted Hamburger?" asked Nell.

The hamburger did not answer.

"That hamburger is so stuck up, he will not even talk to me," said Nell. "I will teach him a lesson."

"Let's race to the hollow log at the edge of the forest. Whoever returns to this stump first will be the winner. On your mark, get set, GO!"

Cousin Nell took off. She flew under the trees and over the rocks. When she reached the hollow log, she smiled. *I know I am faster than a hamburger*, she thought.

But when she returned to the stump, the hamburger
was already there.

"How . . . how . . . how did you get to the log and back
so soon?" panted Nell.

The hamburger was not even out of breath.

"Okay, Hamburger, maybe you are faster. But I know that I
am smarter.

"Owl! Wake up! Ask each of us a math question. We will
see who is smart and who is not."

The owl stretched his wings and yawned.

"What is 7 plus 6?" he asked Nell.

Cousin Nell scribbled some numbers in the dirt. She
scratched her head. She counted on her fingers.

"That is easy," she said. "Seven plus 6 is 452."

"Wrong," said the owl. "Seven plus 6 is 13."

He looked at the hamburger. "Now it is your turn. How much is 12 minus 12?"

The hamburger just sat there.

"That is correct!" said the owl.

"How can that be correct?" asked Nell. "The hamburger said nothing."

"Twelve minus 12 *is* nothing," said the owl. "The hamburger wins!"

Cousin Nell was so mad that she jumped up and down.
"Okay, Hamburger! Maybe you are faster than I am! Maybe you are smarter than I am! But you are not scarier than I am! Look at *this*!"

Cousin Nell crossed her eyes.

She pulled her ears.

She stuck out her tongue.

She wiggled her nose.

"See if you can make a scarier face than *that*, Mr. Haunted Hamburger!"

The hamburger did not move.

"Are you too scared to even try?" She lifted off the top of the bun to make sure that the Haunted Hamburger was listening.

Cousin Nell gasped. She had never seen anything so terrifying in her life.

The hamburger had two round eyes as green as pickles. He had a wide, squiggly mouth as yellow as mustard. He had wet bloody cheeks as red as ketchup.

"Mommmmmmy!" screamed Nell.

She flew back home and hid beneath the table. She did not come out for over two weeks.

Cousin Nell was never a boastful ghost again.

Two round eyes!" said Franny.

"A bloody face!" said Frankie.

"And we thought hot dogs were scary!" they both said.

"Now it is time for bed," said Father Ghost. "Would you like me to tuck you in?"

"Not yet," said Franny. "We want another scary story."

"But I only know one more story," said Father Ghost.

"Tell it! Tell it!" said Franny and Frankie.

"Very well," said Father Ghost. "But I must warn you. This is the scariest story of all. . . ."

The Big Bad Granny

When I was a little ghost I never wanted to go to bed.

"Watch out," warned my father. "If you don't go to bed, you might get a visit from the Big Bad Granny. She is a horrible monster with long skinny arms, sharp pointy fingernails, and terrible, terrible big red lips."

I did not believe him. No one could be that scary.

When my father went to sleep, I climbed out of my bed. I jumped on the chair and swung from the light. "I am never going to sleep," I sang.

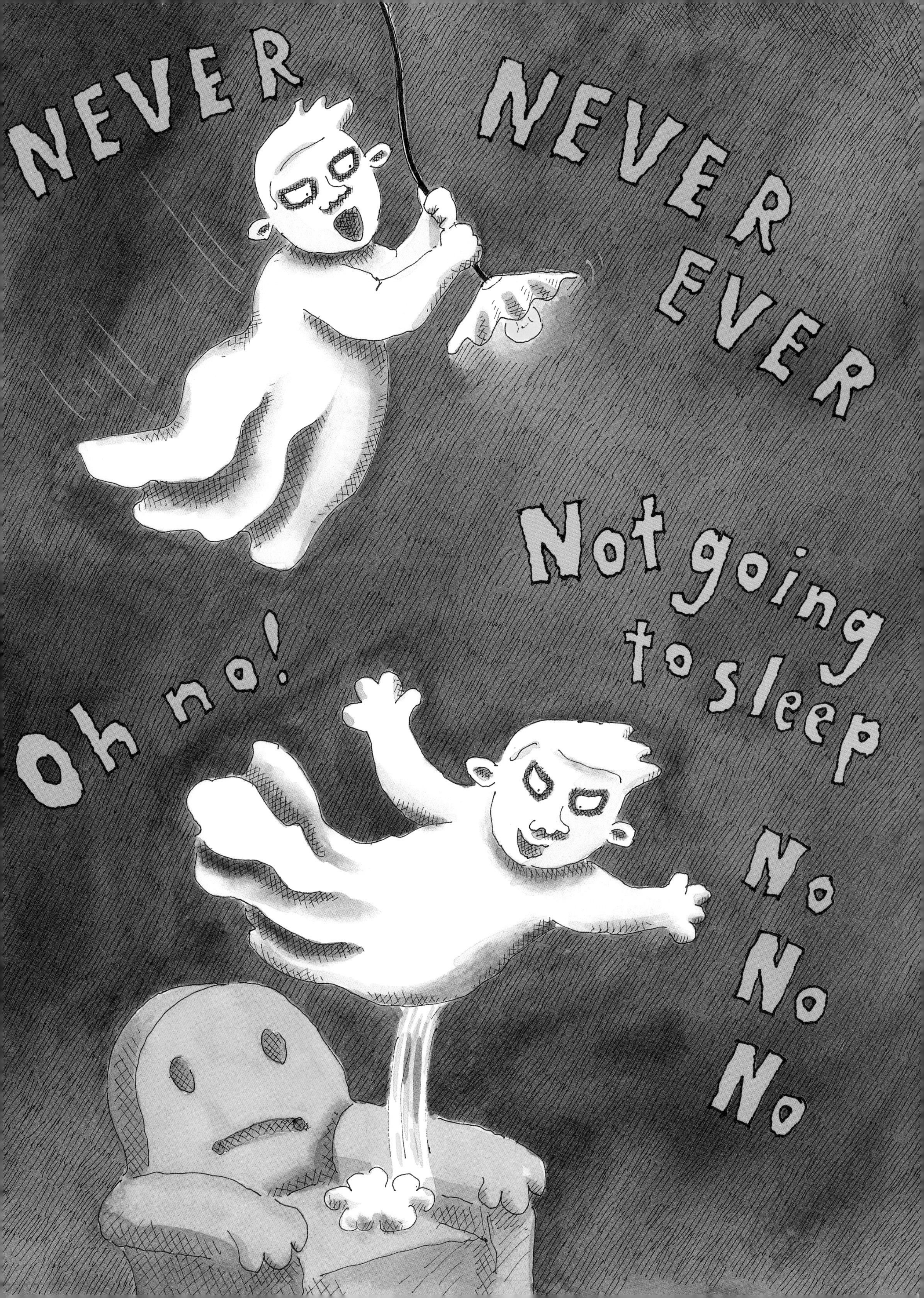

NEVER
NEVER NEVER EVER
Not going to sleep
No No No
Oh no!

**Thump!
Thump!
Thump!**

Thump! Thump! Thump!
Someone was coming up the stairs.
I bet it is our cat, I thought.
"Hee-hee-hee!"
Someone was laughing in the hall.
I bet it is a mouse, I thought.
Click! Click!
The handle to my bedroom door began to turn.
"Father, is that you?" I asked.

The door flew open.
It was the Big Bad Granny!
The Big Bad Granny chased me around my room.

She caught me in her long skinny arms and hugged me until my face turned blue.

Then the Big Bad Granny wiggled her sharp pointy fingernails. She tickled me up and down until my face turned purple.

Finally the Big Bad Granny did the most horrible thing of all.

She smiled her big bad smile, she licked her big red lips . . .

"Don't do it! Don't do it!" I cried.

But the Big Bad Granny kissed me!

She kissed my nose. She kissed my ears. She kissed my neck.
She even kissed my elbows!

I was covered in lipstick for weeks!

H ugging!" cried Franny.

"Tickling!" cried Frankie.

"Kissing!" they both said. "That was the scariest story of all!"

"I hope I have not frightened you too much," said Father Ghost.

"Now it is time to go to sleep."

"More stories! More stories!" cried Franny and Frankie.

"I do not know any more stories," said Father Ghost.

"Then we are going to stay up all night!" said Franny and Frankie.

"Very well," said Father Ghost. "But I am going to bed."

Franny and Frankie bounced on their beds. They hit each other with pillows until . . .

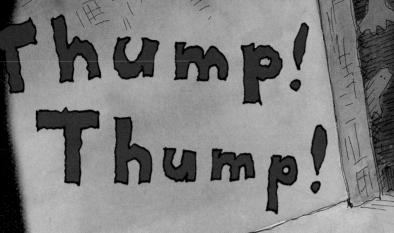

Thump! Thump! Thump!

Someone was climbing up the stairs.

"I bet it is our cat," said Franny.

"We do not have a cat," said Frankie.

"Hee-hee-hee!"

Someone was laughing in the hall.

"I bet it is a mouse," said Franny.

"Mice do not laugh," said Frankie.

Click! Click!

The handle to their bedroom door began to turn.

"It's the Big Bad Granny!" cried Franny and Frankie.

They jumped into bed and closed their eyes.